Cinderella

Lamech Amal Ben Israel

Cinderella

Written by Lamech Amal Ben Israel

Published by Lamech Amal Ben Israel

ISBN:978-0-578-95837-8

"Without a vision, the people perish..."
- King Solomon

"I am black, but comely..."
- King Solomon

Cinderella has a problem. Her father was murdered. Her evil stepmother killed him.

Her stepmother, Madame Idumea, loved being married to Cinderella's father. She wore expensive clothes and jewelry. She also liked that Cinderella's father worked beside the king. She always liked to tell Cinderella's father what new rules to suggest.

But the king didn't like that Cinderella's father let her stepmother have so much influence over his actions. Also, to marry a woman who was not of their race and nation was against their laws. So, the king fired Cinderella's father, until he learned to properly order his household.

Cinderella's father had lost his money and his power. Madame Idumea didn't like that. So, she killed him. She would have killed Cinderella, too. But the king and Cinderella's father were good friends. So, when he heard Cinderella's father was dead, he sent money to be used for her care. Cinderella's stepmother liked getting money and kept it. But she moved Cinderella away, in case anyone came to look for her. She also had the money sent to a special mailbox. That way, no one would know she had Cinderella.

Also, Cinderella's name is not, "Cinderella." Her name is Zion. Her cruel and evil stepsisters just called her "Cinderella" to make fun of her. "Cinderella" means "ash beauty" or "little ashes."
"Because your skin looks like it was burned to ash," they said.
Her stepsisters didn't like Cinderella's skin-color. They didn't like anything about her.

Because Zion's name was changed to "Cinderella" and she was moved out of town, the king could not find her. This was a problem, because Zion was supposed to marry the prince. Zion, who is Cinderella, and the prince were looking forward to the marriage.

Then the prince had an idea.
"I will throw a party in the town," the prince said. "All the people will come. And at the party, I will find Zion."

Now, in the town, Cinderella is out shopping with her stepmother and stepsisters. She has to carry all the bags. Then, a messenger tells the town that the prince is hosting a party at the Grand hall.

Cinderella hasn't seen royalty or a royal party in a long time. Surely, if she appeared, someone would recognize her. She asks her stepmother if she can go. Her stepmother says, "No."

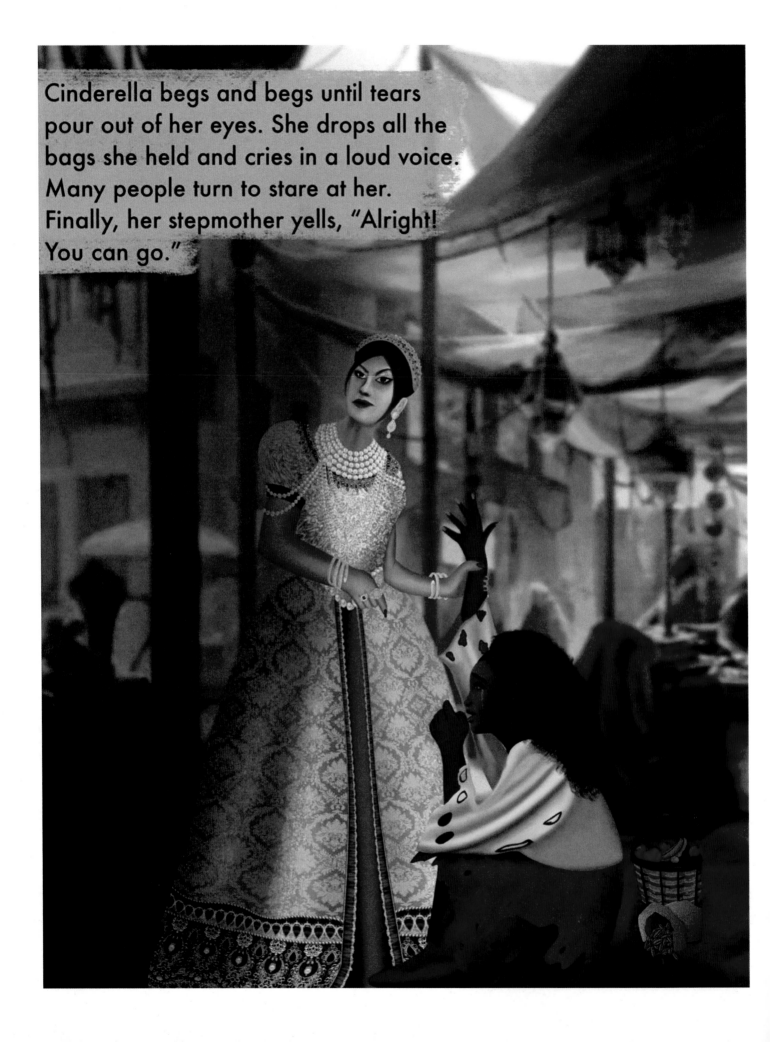

Cinderella begs and begs until tears pour out of her eyes. She drops all the bags she held and cries in a loud voice. Many people turn to stare at her. Finally, her stepmother yells, "Alright! You can go."

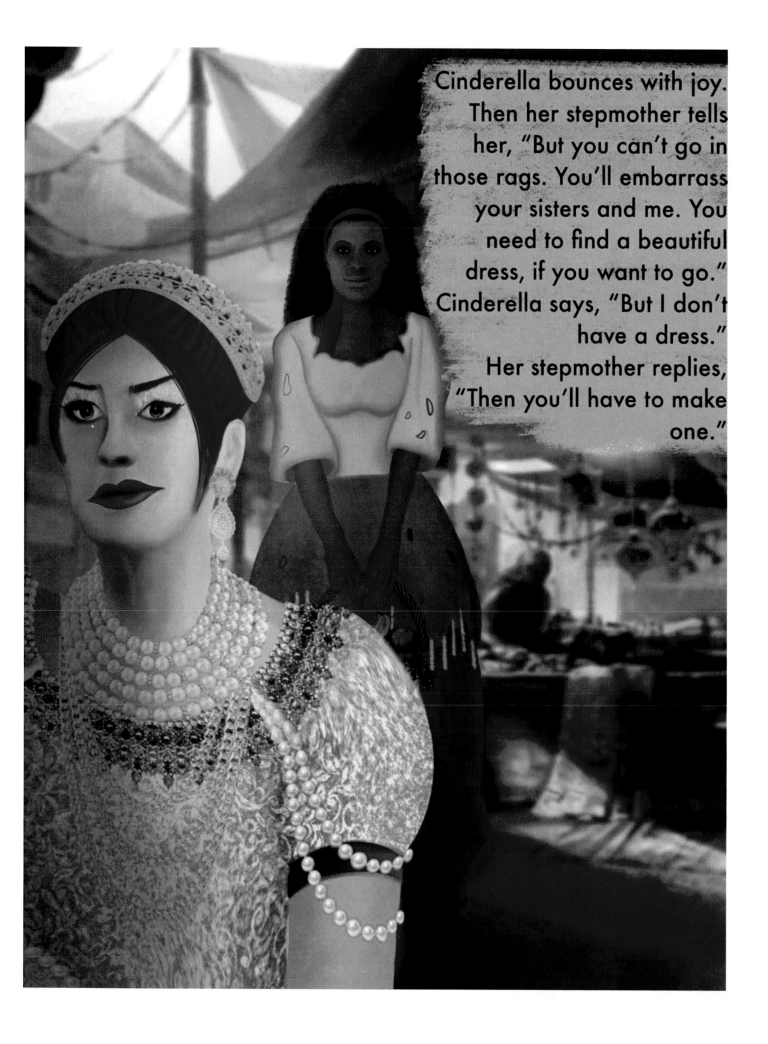

Cinderella bounces with joy. Then her stepmother tells her, "But you can't go in those rags. You'll embarrass your sisters and me. You need to find a beautiful dress, if you want to go." Cinderella says, "But I don't have a dress." Her stepmother replies, "Then you'll have to make one."

Cinderella goes home and gets to work on making a dress. She goes under bed and pulls out a book left by her father. She opens it to a page that explains how a lady should dress. Then, she pulls out a thread and needles to sew her dress together.

Her stepmother and stepsisters see her
sewing.
The older stepsister asks, "Do we really
have to take her with us, Mother?"
The younger stepsister says, "Yeah. I
don't want to be seen with her."
"No, dearies," their mother says. "I just
said that to give her something to do
while we leave her."
So, they sneak away and leave
Cinderella.

Cinderella finishes her dress, just before sundown. But when she goes to tell her stepmother, she finds that she is gone. "They must have gone without me," Cinderella says. "I'll just have to go to the party by myself."
So, she looks for a way to go to the party and finds a horse. "I know. I'll ride this horse to the party," Cinderella says. She hops on the horse and rides away.

When she gets to the party, Cinderella jumps off the horse and runs into the Grand Hall. When her evil stepmother and stepsisters see her, they are very angry. They follow Cinderella, to see if they can find her alone.

Cinderella, tired from riding a horse, goes to the restroom to wipe her face. Her evil stepmother and stepsisters follow her and trap her. They tear her beautiful dress apart and leave Cinderella alone and sobbing.

The prince arrives and tells everyone that he threw this party to find Zion. I haven't seen her in a while," the prince says, "but I'll know here when I see her."

Cinderella's stepsisters go to the prince and claim to be Zion. The older wears a tight skirt that stops above her knees. The younger is wearing pants. The prince says, "Neither of you can be her. A person is known by look and clothing. I know Zion was taught to look and dress more like a lady."

Cinderella creeps from the shadows and sees the prince. The prince sees her, but she dashes behind a pillar.

"Come on out," the prince calls. "Let me see you."

Cinderella takes a deep breath and walks out into the light.

Her stepmother says, "This can't be the girl you want. See how dirty she is and how her clothes are torn? She has no respect for your majesty."

But the prince says, "No. See, this woman has fringes at the end of her dress. And they are laced with a blue ribband. Only those of the king's court were taught this."

The prince approaches Cinderella. He says, "I am the prince and the one who ordered this party. What is your name? And why do you have fringes?" Cinderella says, "I am Zion of Israel. My father had left me a book that commanded to wear fringes at the border of my clothes. He was once a member of the king's court."

The prince was very happy to hear this. "I have found you, Zion," he said. "Where is your father? And why is your dress torn?"

Cinderella, whose name is Zion, said, "He was murdered. Murdered by the same people who tore my dress."

When the prince heard this, he was very angry. "Who did this?" he asked. "I demand to know!"

Zion points to her stepmother and stepsisters.

Before the stepmother and stepsisters could run, the guards grab them and arrest them. The prince tells them, "Because you have killed Zion's father and done evil things to Zion, you also will die."

The guards take the evil stepmother and stepsisters away.

Cinderella, whose name is Zion, marries the prince. Now, no one calls her, "Cinderella." Instead, they call her, "Princess Zion." And no one makes her afraid or is mean to her. All because she never gave up, she kept her honesty, and she acted and dressed like a lady. Even when her life was torn apart.

Lamech Amal Ben Israel is a screenwriter, novelist, and short-story writer who creates inspirational fiction designed to empower Blacks, Hispanics, Native Americans and their kin scattered through colonialism and slavery, who have been historically marginalized and stigmatized. Israel's first and middle names, Lamech Amal, mean "powerful" and "determination," respectively, simply meaning, "I can, and I will."

His trademark stories, with their complex superheroes, compelling plot twists, and fantasy settings, instill the same "I can, and I will" attitude in his readers. Lamech Israel is a graduate of Full Sail University with a Master of Fine Arts in Creative Writing. When he is not writing, Israel enjoys studying history, engaging in the arts, studying languages, acquiring new skills, and planning to recreate the world.